No Trace

No Trace

Brenda Chapman

Anna Sweet Mysteries
GRASS ROOTS PRESS

First published in 2016 by Grass Roots Press

We acknowledge the financial support of the Government of Canada.

Produced with the assistance of the Government of Alberta,
Alberta Multimedia Development Fund.

Government

Library and Archives Canada Cataloguing in Publication

Chapman, Brenda, 1955–, author
    No trace / Brenda Chapman.

(Anna Sweet)
ISBN 978–1–77153–008–8 (paperback)

    I. Title. II. Series.

PS8605.H36N6 2016   C813'.6   C2016–902586–1

Printed and bound in Canada.

MIX
Paper from
responsible sources
FSC
www.fsc.org   FSC® C103214

For Ted

Dad pulled me out of a deep sleep Sunday morning with the smell of frying bacon and dark roasted coffee. I rolled over in my single bed and moaned. My head felt as if a lawn mower was plowing its way through my brain.

I'd put in a late night working on a case. An insurance company had hired me to find out if a city bus driver's bad back claim was true. I'd followed the man to Montreal, where he helped his daughter move out of her apartment. The bus driver spent the next six hours drinking in a bar down the street. After a few beers, he'd shown some fancy moves on the dance floor. Just in case the photos of him dragging a sofa down two flights of stairs weren't enough.

When the bus driver finally stumbled to his hotel, I made the two and a half hour drive home to my bed in Ottawa, arriving just after five a.m.

"You up, Anna?" Dad yelled from the kitchen. He banged a pot on the stove. "Thought you might like some breakfast."

I moaned again and rolled onto my side, slowly opening one eye to look at the clock. *Eight thirty.* That meant I'd been in bed exactly three and a half hours. I shut my eye again. I tried to focus on breathing in and out. Dad was working through his worries about my sister Cheri and her marriage problems by cooking day and night. My stomach could hardly take any more new recipes. My head needed more sleep.

"I'll be right there!" I called. I put the pillow over my head. "Just five more minutes," I mumbled.

I'd nicely drifted off when my cellphone rang on the dresser.

"Nooooo," I groaned. What had I done to make the world turn against me?

After closing my eyes for a moment, I tossed the pillow onto the floor and pushed myself out of bed. I grabbed the phone and hit receive before it went to voice mail. I almost dropped the phone from the shock of hearing Detective Johnny Shaw's voice growl into my ear.

"That you, Sweet?"

"Maybe." After a pause, I said, "I'm surprised you're working on a Sunday." I had no idea what he wanted but knew it had to be something important.

"Not as surprised as I am." He sighed loudly. "Wonder if you could come by the station this morning. There's somebody who needs your help."

The smell of sizzling bacon was making my mouth water. I could hear Dad beating eggs in a bowl. "I can be there in an hour," I said. "I have some, uh, business to take care of first."

Shaw gave another drawn-out sigh. "I can wait. Even though my kids and I are supposed to be on the ski hill, enjoying the day."

I said with fake sympathy, "I'm sorry, but sometimes we all have to take one for the team. I'll be there as soon as I can."

I hung up and grabbed my housecoat. Shaw really was a piece of work. I knew for a fact that he didn't have any kids. And the picture of his bear-sized body shooting gracefully down a ski hill was enough to make me laugh out loud.

Plus, the ski hills weren't open for the season yet.

I needed time to fully wake up. I'd have a quick shower and try to clear my head before making my way to the kitchen. Whatever Shaw wanted could wait for me to have a couple of cups of coffee and a plate of bacon and eggs—even if his call made me as curious as a cat in a room full of mouse holes.

· · · · · · · · · ·

I smelled snow in the late-November morning. The leaves had fallen from the trees weeks before and lay soggy and brown on the lawn. For once, I was looking forward to winter. Snow would be better than the damp, chilly days we'd had all month. For weeks on end the sun had been hiding behind low grey clouds, and people were as depressed as I'd ever seen them.

Shaw was waiting for me in his office at the Elgin Street police station, but he wasn't alone. My brother-in-law, Jimmy Wilson, was leaning against the wall drinking a cup of coffee. He was wearing jeans and a soft brown leather jacket and had the beginnings of a beard that hinted of the rugged outdoors. I couldn't remember the last time I'd seen him looking so relaxed. Cheri told me that he'd been going to the gym, and he appeared to have lost weight and toned up.

A middle-aged man and woman were seated in two visitor chairs, and there was an empty one next to the woman. As I stepped past them, I noticed the beautiful jade-coloured silk scarf tied loosely around the woman's neck. Her eyes were large behind bright, blue-framed glasses, and she wore a black beret tilted to one side of her head, covering greying curls. Her husband sat taller next to her, a watchful man with a bald head and long face that reminded me of a hound dog. She'd shredded a tissue in her lap and white bits covered her coat like flakes of dandruff. I nodded at them before sitting down.

Shaw's pale blue eyes met mine. He cleared his throat. "Anna Sweet, meet Vanda and Chuck Green. Their son has been missing six months. I think it is time to get a PI involved. The Greens have agreed to hire you."

Shaw closed his mouth as if this was all that needed saying. The Greens and I stared at each other. Vanda's eyes filled with tears. Chuck looked down at his hands. I reached into my pocket and pulled out a pen and a notebook. "What can you tell me about your son?" I asked.

Vanda looked at Chuck and he held her eyes for a moment. Some silent struggle appeared to be going on between them. Finally, Chuck turned sideways and looked at me.

"Ryan is seventeen and in grade twelve...well, he would be if he wasn't missing. He was a student at Brookfield High School and planned to become a carpenter. Not sure what else you want to know, exactly."

"Do you have other children, Mr. Green?"

"We have another son. Travis is sixteen and also goes to Brookfield. We live in Ottawa South, not far from the canal."

"We've been frantic," Vanda said, loud enough to signal that she was close to losing control. "Just frantic. Ryan would never disappear without letting us know where he was going. I need to know where he is, even if the worst has happened to him." Her voice was rising to a dangerous level. "I need to know if he's dead or alive!"

Her words rang like a big dose of panic in our ears. Shaw leaned forward in his chair. He rubbed his forehead and spoke before the silence stretched too long. "I have a full file for you to read, Sweet. Why don't you go through it and get an idea what's been going on. Officer Wilson is here to help bring you up to speed. I'm sure Chuck and Vanda will be eager to speak with you afterward."

I nodded and said to the Greens, "I'll put everything else aside to work on finding your son." I was doing my part to help Shaw head off Vanda's total breakdown.

Jimmy gave me a half-smile that I ignored. We hadn't spoken since he and Cheri took a break from their marriage. I knew he was living in a bachelor apartment down the road in Westboro, a popular Ottawa neighbourhood near my PI office. My sister and their seven-year-old son Evan were renting a town house near my dad's place in Alta Vista. I added, "I'll let you know if I have any questions, Officer Wilson."

"I'm here for you, Sweet." Again, with the sleepy half-smile. The way Jimmy looked at me let me know that he wanted to start back up with me. He couldn't seem to grasp that dumping me to marry my sister had been a deal breaker.

I stood up and shook the Greens' hands before picking up their son's file from the desk. "I'll be in touch within a day or two," I said.

"We really hope you can help us," Vanda said. Her bottom lip trembled but she kept her voice level. "All we want is for Ryan to come home. Even if he did something wrong and ran away, we forgive him. If you find him, make sure you tell him that."

CHAPTER TWO

I drove to the office I shared with Jada Price on Wellington Street, in a section of the city named Hintonburg. We'd set up our PI business above a pizza restaurant. The owner, Gino Roma, waved me inside when he saw me walking past.

The familiar spicy mix of tomato sauce, garlic and oregano filled my senses when I stepped through the door. Gino wiped his hands on his apron as he came toward me for a hug. "How's our girl?" he asked, his smile as wide as a slice of one of his pizzas.

"Good, Gino. I'm good." I held up the file folder. "I have a new police case to help investigate. Never a dull moment."

He stepped back and looked me over. His black eyes saw something that worried him. Like Dad, his answer to any problem was forcing food on me. "I just this minute made a pepperoni and double cheese pizza. I'll put it into a box for you to take upstairs. You look tired. You need to eat."

"Thanks, Gino."

He went behind the counter and picked up a piece of cardboard, which he expertly formed into a box. Then he reached into the wood-burning oven and took out a pizza, glancing at me as he boxed it up and set it on the counter. "So, any word from my Nicky?"

"Not for a week. He's busy filming." I'd recently started dating Nick Roma, who was also our office assistant at Storm Investigations. That is, when he wasn't being a movie star.

"Shouldn't be too busy to call his girlfriend…or his family."

"He'll be in touch when he has time." I picked up the pizza box. "I'll see you later, Gino."

"You're probably right. I'll let you know if I hear from him. Don't work too hard, Anna."

I left the restaurant and climbed the steps to our office. Jada was on vacation in Bermuda and not due back for another week. She'd said that she had to escape our rainy November weather or she'd go out of her mind. With Jada away and Nick in Vancouver filming a movie, I had the office and the pizza all to myself. I was surprised how much I missed the two of them.

I brewed a pot of coffee in our machine then sat at my desk and started in on the pizza. I opened the file and began reading as I ate.

Ryan Green was last seen leaving his school after English class on May 30. That morning he told his mother he was staying late for soccer practice. But his coach got sick and practice was cancelled. Ryan's grades were average and school staff said that he was more interested in sports than academics. He also had a part-time job at an auto dealership, working behind the counter. He'd started dating a girl from another school but no one had met her yet. Everybody liked Ryan and said he was easy-going and friendly.

His best friend, Ben Draper, said that Ryan wasn't into drugs, although they drank beer now and then. They liked to party, but no more than other kids their age. He had no idea what could have happened to his friend. Ben was the last person to see Ryan the day he went missing.

Vanda and Chuck had also been interviewed, separately and together. Ryan's mom was frantic from the start. She said that something terrible must have happened to keep her son from calling home. Chuck was worried as well, but thought Ryan could look after himself if he had to. But he was less and less certain as the days passed. Neither had any idea where Ryan could have gone.

Ryan's sixteen-year-old brother, Travis, said that he had no idea where Ryan could be. He and Ryan were close but he hadn't known about the new girlfriend. He wasn't sure she even existed. Nothing had been bothering Ryan that he knew about.

I picked up Ryan's photo, which was paper clipped to the back of the folder. He was a good-looking boy, with a sweet smile and sky blue eyes. He wore his black hair longer on top than on the sides. His profile said that he was five foot ten, 155 pounds.

"Where are you, Ryan Green?" I asked, staring into his eyes and hoping for an answer.

Sighing, I picked up my empty coffee cup and thought about one last refill. My cellphone rang at that moment and I set the cup back down. I'd probably had enough caffeine anyway. Jimmy's number popped up.

"Want to meet up, Sweet? I have an hour free."

I glanced at my watch. Three o'clock and not much time left in the day to start interviews. People would soon be sitting down to Sunday dinner. I still had a pile of reading to do about the day Ryan went missing, but Jimmy could fill me in a lot faster. "Sure. How about we meet at Whispers Pub in twenty minutes?"

"I'll be there."

....

Jimmy was sitting at a table for two by the window when I arrived. He'd ordered two pints of beer and he tilted his glass in my direction after I sat down.

"You've been given an impossible file," he said. "Ryan Green disappeared without a trace."

"Someone has to know something."

"You'd think." Jimmy pulled a notepad from the inside pocket of his leather jacket. "But I couldn't find anybody who saw him that afternoon after he left school."

"Nobody?"

"Nobody. He left soon after finding out soccer practice was cancelled." Jimmy checked his notes. "At three twenty, he met up with his buddy Ben Draper at their lockers. They walked out the front door together but parted ways on the sidewalk. Ryan never made it home. He vanished into thin air."

"Ryan didn't have a car?"

"He sometimes drove his mom's car but he was on foot that day."

"What about his mystery girlfriend? Did he tell anyone her name?"

"No, but his brother Travis said that wasn't unusual. Ryan dated a lot of different girls but rarely brought them home. I checked out every name the family came up with. None of the girls saw him that day outside of school."

"It sounds like he didn't care about their feelings much. A bit of a rat, if you ask me."

"More like young and hard to pin down. Everyone said that Ryan lived moment to moment. He was often late and forgetful because he'd get caught up in what he was doing. Everyone knew he wasn't completely dependable, but nobody held it against him. All in all, he was a popular kid."

"Did these girls know about each other?" I admit that I was having trouble letting the multiple girlfriend angle go.

"They did, but they all said that they weren't in serious relationships. They were all unaware he was seeing someone new, though."

"Now, that seems a bit odd to me."

"She must have meant something to Ryan if he wanted to keep her to himself." Jimmy stared at me until I looked away.

Why was I having so much trouble feeling nothing for this man? He'd left me for my sister, after all. My voice came out grumpy. "So you have no suspects or leads?"

"Nope. Nada. Ryan didn't make any calls on his cellphone after he left school that day. I'd say the phone was destroyed, because the signal couldn't be found to trace it. Needless to say, we never found a body."

"This is one strange case."

Jimmy gave me a sideways grin. "Very strange. I hope you can find something we missed, but I'm not holding my breath, Sweet."

"That makes two of us, Officer Wilson."

CHAPTER THREE

I drove through the darkened streets toward Dad's place. I'd thought about going back to the office but didn't feel like being alone. I longed to see Nick's face and feel his arms around me. I needed him more than I would ever let on. *Why didn't he call?*

I smelled roast beef and gravy when I stepped inside the back door. Dad was stirring something in a pot on the stove and singing along to the radio. He didn't see me come into the kitchen and I watched him for a moment from the doorway. His eyes were closed and he was swaying in time to the song.

"Hey, Dad," I said softly so as not to startle him. "Smells good in here."

He opened his eyes and for a moment, he seemed to be reliving something in the past. It took him a few seconds to come back to the present. He raised the spoon out of the pot and pointed it in my direction. "You're late. Cheri and Evan should be here any minute. I need you to set the table." His voice was gruff but his eyes still shone with whatever good memory my entrance had interrupted.

I turned to hang up my coat and to give Dad some time. Then I started to take out knives and forks and plates to set the table. "Is Betty joining us tonight?" I asked. Dad had met Betty at a dance studio in September and they'd been seeing each other ever since.

"No. She's busy. Just the four of us."

"That's too bad."

I wasn't sure that I was up for an evening with my sister. But I kept quiet. Cheri and Evan arrived a few minutes later, and Dad had us sitting around the table as soon as they had their coats off. He served up homemade rolls to go with the roast, mashed potatoes, homemade brown beans, and coleslaw. Dessert was a lemon sponge cake with raspberries and whipped cream. After the last bite of cake, I set down my fork and undid the top button on my jeans. I promised myself that I'd set the alarm to get up early for a run.

Evan and Cheri had been unusually silent during the meal. I could tell by the way Dad was watching them that he was trying to figure out what was going on. I got up to make tea and Evan came with me to help. I could hear Dad asking Cheri her plans for the week.

Evan rubbed against my arm. "Mommy has a new boyfriend," he said.

I looked down into his worried face. "Maybe he's just a friend."

"No. He sleeps over when I'm at Dad's. Some of his clothes are in Mommy's closet." Evan picked up the mugs I'd set on the counter. He whispered, "I found his toothbrush and shaving stuff in the bathroom cupboard."

I glanced at Cheri through the open doorway. She was looking at me with a questioning look on her face. But I knew she couldn't have heard what Evan had said.

"How do you feel about that?" I asked my seven-year-old nephew. I knew how I felt and it wasn't happy.

"I was hoping we could move back in with Dad."

I bent down and pulled him into a hug. "We all want that, kiddo. But it's between your parents. You and I can't change things just because we want to." I pulled back. Evan's big blue eyes, so like my sister's, looked into mine without blinking.

"At least Mommy doesn't cry all the time anymore."

I pulled him to me again.

After the tea, Cheri and Evan left, and I cleaned up the kitchen. Dad went to read in his bedroom. It felt as if the grey November days had worked their way into our home. I was happy to have a case to take my mind off my family's problems. I'd begin interviews in the morning and would hopefully lose myself in the mystery of Ryan Green's disappearance.

It was going to take a lot of long hours at work to get the look that I'd seen in Evan's eyes out of my head.

· · · · · · · · · ·

The sun took its sweet time rising on these November mornings. I jogged the side streets in darkness at six a.m., a brisk wind making me fight to catch my breath on the way home. A hot shower followed by two cups of coffee warmed me up. While I waited for Dad to get out of bed, I spread Ryan's file out on the kitchen table and read through the rest of the documents. At eight thirty, I made some phone calls to set up interviews. Dad finally came into the kitchen in his housecoat and slippers as I was putting on my coat.

"Did you eat breakfast?" he asked.

"I'm still full from supper. I'll pick something up later."

"Fast food." He spit the two words out as if trying to clear a bad taste. He crossed to the counter and poured a cup of coffee. "I must have been tired. I can't remember the last time I got up this late."

"You're allowed. This weather makes me want to crawl into bed for a week." I took a cap from my pocket and pulled it over my hair, which was still damp from the shower. "I'm not sure if I'll be home for supper. I hope Betty can eat my share."

"Not unless I airlift the food to Florida. She's rented a condo and should be halfway to Miami by now."

I paused with my hand on the doorknob. "I was getting used to seeing her here for meals. When will she be back?"

"Not sure." Dad frowned at me. "Shouldn't you be getting a move on?"

I wanted to stay and find out how he felt about Betty leaving, and about Cheri... being Cheri. But he was right. I had to get moving.

"I'll try to get home for supper, Dad," I said.

He rewarded me with a quick smile before his face returned to its normal stern default. "Well now," he said, sitting down at the table with his iPad. He put on his reading glasses. "Let me just see if I can rustle us up a new recipe."

I stepped outside into the pale morning light. If I managed to get all the interviews over early, I'd have time to look into buying a gym membership on my way home. That or invest in a bigger pair of jeans.

CHAPTER FOUR

B en Draper was a tall, skinny kid with curly brown hair and a shy smile. I liked him right off but I knew that everyone had secrets and Ben would be no different.

He invited me into the kitchen and we sat at the table in front of the patio doors. The Drapers had a big back yard with lots of oak trees. Nobody had bothered to rake up the brown leaves that covered the ground like a thick blanket.

"Thanks for seeing me," I said.

"I have half an hour before I have to leave for class."

"We should be done in lots of time. You were best friends with Ryan. What can you tell me about him?"

"He's a great guy. We met in grade nine, the same year that the Greens moved into Ottawa South."

"I see they live three blocks over from you."

"I met Ryan playing soccer and then we started hanging out. He said they moved around a lot before his dad took a desk job here."

"His mom works from home, according to the police file."

"Yeah, she's an artist and kind of emotional. She's over the top crazy when it comes to Ryan and Travis."

"How so?"

"Like, she's really involved in their lives. I mean to the extreme. Poor Travis can't make a move now. She's always phoning him and checking up. I don't know how he stands it."

His comment opened up a new line of thought for me. "Do you think Ryan would take off to get away from his mother?"

"I would have." Ben laughed. "Ryan seemed used to it, though. He was always calling her when we were out and leaving early to make curfew. He said keeping her happy was easier than dealing with her hundred and one questions later."

"How about his dad? Did they get along?"

Ben shrugged. "From what Ryan told me, his dad wasn't around a lot when he was a kid. The last few years, his dad came out to our soccer games but he never said very much to us before or after the game."

"Before Ryan went missing, was there any sign that he was planning to leave town?"

"No. He was happy to have a few hours open up when soccer practice was cancelled. He didn't tell his mom it was cancelled, though. I know that."

"Why not? Where was he going?"

"He never said."

"You must have had an idea." I stared at him until he couldn't stand it any longer and started talking.

"If I had to guess back then, I'd have said he was meeting a girlfriend. Nobody came forward, though, so who knows?" Ben checked the clock on the wall. "I should get moving. Do you have any more questions?" A red flush had spread from his neck up his cheeks.

"Yeah. Did you go straight home after you left Ryan?"

Ben blinked as if he hadn't expected the question. He took his time answering. "I met some friends in a study group in the library."

"Names?"

"I can't remember now. Is it important?"

"Maybe not." And maybe yes.

I stood when he did. I was curious why he was suddenly so eager for me to leave. But I couldn't make him late for school. I said, "That ought to do it for now. Here's my card if you think of anything that might help."

Ben took the card and put it into the back pocket of his jeans. "I have no idea what that would be, but I'll call if anything comes up."

He followed me to the front door and shut it after me with a solid bang.

· · · · · · · · · ·

My next stop was Brookfield High School. I'd booked some time with the principal and was sent straight into her office when I arrived. It wasn't the first time that I'd been sent to the principal's office, but happily, the other times were well in my past. Even so, I felt sweat forming on my forehead and around the collar of my jacket.

Mrs. Gibbons stood and shook my hand. We took seats at a table loaded down with files and textbooks. She was tall with intelligent brown eyes and red hair pulled back into a bun. She poured us each a cup of hot coffee from a thermos.

"Ryan Green has caused me many a sleepless night," she said. "When he first went missing, I kept wondering if we'd done something different... well, maybe he'd still be here."

"What do you think happened to him?"

"I'm not lying when I say that I have no idea." She took a sip of coffee. "I carried on my own investigation soon after he disappeared. Nobody saw him after he left school property. He might have gotten into a car with somebody. We just don't know."

"What kind of student was Ryan?"

"Not too engaged, except when it came to sports, shop class, or girls. He was polite, well liked, and respectful. A good kid, I'd say."

"Did he have any problems? Was something or someone bothering him?"

Mrs. Gibbons shook her head. "Nobody noticed anything, if that was the case. And none of my teachers could think of any reason he'd run away. I'm completely at a loss as to where he could be...I pray every day that he's still alive."

There was a knock at the door and Ryan's brother, Travis, stepped into the office. Mrs. Gibbons stood and patted him on the shoulder. Her voice became loud and jolly. "There you are, Travis. Good of you to take this little break from class."

"I don't mind."

"I'll bet you don't. I imagine your teacher was about to check homework. We'll have you back in no time." She laughed, a deep, rumbling sound. "Take my seat. I have to go speak to a grade nine class before letting them loose on a field trip. Nice meeting you, Ms. Sweet. If I can be of further help, don't hesitate to be in touch."

"Thank you." I waited until Travis was seated and took the time to look him over. He had the same good looks as his brother, although he was slimmer with darker hair and eyes.

"Thanks for meeting me," I began. "I'm sorry to hear about Ryan and know how hard this must be for you."

"Yeah, it's been tough." Travis slumped back in the chair. "I have no idea where he could be," he shrugged, "or why he left."

I took a second to watch him. Something felt off. The sad frown on his lips didn't reach his eyes. "Did you get along with Ryan?" I asked. I studied him while I waited.

"Sure, we got along. He didn't tell me he was planning to leave, if that's what you're thinking."

"So, you had no idea that something might be wrong?"

"Nope."

"Were you close enough that he would have told you?"

"Yeah, I guess." Travis ran a hand across his jaw. "But he didn't."

Man, this kid was going out of his way to tell me that he didn't know anything. His denials were making me curious. Time to shake him up a bit. "Have you heard from Ryan since he left?" I asked quietly. "Because you don't seem as upset as I would have thought you'd be. "

Travis shook his head and glared at me. "You've got it wrong. I'm as worried as my parents about Ryan." He jumped out of the seat. He was halfway to the door when he turned and said, "I've got to get back to class. You can talk to my parents if you want to know anything else about my brother."

I let him go. It was clear that he wasn't going to tell me anything more, even if he had something to share. When I left the office, Mrs. Gibbons was nowhere in sight. I exited the school by the front door and decided to grab some lunch and review my notes before making it to my next meeting.

CHAPTER FIVE

Ryan had worked some evenings and Saturdays at the Frankie's Ford dealership on Walkley Road at Bank Street. It was a fair distance from the school but could be walked in forty minutes or so. Had Ryan started out in that direction the day he disappeared?

I drove the most direct route before cruising around the side streets near the dealership. The Bella Vista Restaurant was a block over in a strip mall with a grocery store at one end. I tried to put myself in Ryan's shoes. Had he stopped to eat at the Bella Vista between school and work? I pulled into the parking lot. The hunch was worth checking out.

I took a seat in a booth and a pleasant-looking woman soon approached. She was in her fifties, with curled white-blonde hair and a trim shape under her gold uniform. The place was a family-run restaurant, known for its pizza, but I ordered a cheeseburger platter and coffee. Eating another cook's pizza would have felt wrong, as if I was two-timing on Gino.

I looked around while I waited. The decor was cream and black with rust-coloured wood in the floor and ceiling beams. Nothing fancy and no need to feel out of place in my jeans and plaid shirt. This was the kind of place where a teenage kid would grab a bite to eat.

The woman came back with my coffee. I read her name tag as I pulled a photo of Ryan out of my jacket and held it out to her. "Do you know this young man, Jeannie?" I asked.

She glanced at the photo and then held it closer for another look. She smiled. "Why, that's Ryan. He used to come in here after school before his shift at Frankie's. He hasn't been in for a while, though." Her face changed from friendly to suspicious. "Can I ask why you're showing me his picture?"

"His family hasn't seen him in about six months. They have no idea where he could be. You hadn't heard that the police were looking for him?"

She shook her head. "No. I don't follow the news much because it's always so depressing. The police never came to the restaurant. I hope Ryan's okay. He's a nice kid."

"Was he ever with anybody when he came in to eat?"

Jeannie squinted at me through her glasses. "Who did you say you were again?"

"I'm private investigator Anna Sweet. Ryan's parents hired me to find him."

She glanced down at my ID card and back up at my face. Her mouth settled into a straight line, turned down at the ends. "I didn't see him with anybody. Now, if you'll excuse me..." She turned without waiting for me to answer and disappeared into the kitchen.

A few minutes later, a young man served my food. Jeannie didn't come out of the kitchen again, which seemed odd. I finished eating and paid my bill, still with no sign of her. Was she avoiding me or had she gone off shift? I had no way of knowing, but the curious feeling that started with Ben and Travis was starting to grow.

··········

The front lot of Frankie's Ford took up a city block, showing off the latest shiny new cars and trucks. The back of the property was reserved for used models. I found a parking spot near a row of garage doors where a team of mechanics serviced Ford vehicles. It was a large operation and the leather couches in the waiting room made it clear Frankie's was making money. There was even an expensive coffee maker in the corner under a big screen television with a sign that said to help yourself.

I walked up to the counter. I pictured Ryan Green standing here when he worked after school and on weekends. A white-haired man in navy work clothes was on duty. His name tag said *Carl*. He took his time getting up from his chair behind the counter to shuffle over to me.

"Yeah, can I help you?"

"I hope so. I'm private investigator Anna Sweet and I've been hired to look into Ryan Green's disappearance. Did you know him?"

"Of course I did, young lady. If he hadn't taken off without a word, I'd be working in the garage where I belong. We're short-staffed in there too. Too many people just up and leaving without giving proper notice."

I leaned on the counter and tried to look friendly. "Any idea why he took off?"

"Who knows? Kids these days. Heads always bent over some electronic gadget. Don't know how to hold a conversation or the meaning of a good day's work."

"It seems odd the owner hasn't replaced Ryan by now."

"Nothing odd about it. You're looking at the owner."

It took a minute to compute. "But your name's Carl."

"That's right. I'm Carl Montana. Frankie Montana was my father. He handed the business down to me and my son Bobby gets his turn when I die." He looked toward the door. Through the window, I could see the garage and mechanics working on cars and trucks. Carl moved closer. "Bobby thinks he's in charge now and he will be soon enough. He can have the headaches. Letting your son take over is one of the perks of getting old." He grinned and his brown eyes twinkled.

I found myself liking him. "So you work on the cars?"

"I do. Never much enjoyed the business side. As to replacing Ryan, Bobby's daughter Maggie usually works today, but she's got exams. She's a student at Carleton University. Smart girl."

The door banged open and a younger, more muscular version of Carl entered, wiping his hands on an oil rag. By the bit of grey in his black hair, he looked to be in his fifties. "Hey, Pops. Everything okay?"

"Yeah, son. This here's Anna Sweet, PI. She's trying to find out what happened to young Ryan."

Bobby's eyes went from me to his dad and back again. His eyes were deep green and his stare was piercing. He laughed. "I'd offer you a hand to shake but mine are a bit dirty." His face went serious. "We sure are worried about Ryan. I wish we had something to tell you that could help bring him home. Let his parents know we're here if they need our help in any way."

"Thanks, I'll be sure to tell them. Did he come by the garage the day he went missing?"

"No. The police asked us the same question."

"I'm going over the facts, trying to retrace Ryan's steps that day. Here's my business card if you remember anything, although I know it's been a while."

Carl picked up the card where I'd put it on the counter. "Thanks, young lady. How did you get into this dangerous line of work, anyhow?"

"Dad, that's none of our business," said Bobby. His voice was sharp and Carl looked down at the card in his hand.

Bobby smiled widely at me. "Please forgive my dad. I'm afraid he comes from a time when women were secretaries, teachers, or home with the kids."

"Not really all that long ago," I said. "Well, thanks for your help." I started toward the entrance but stopped and turned with my hand on the door. Both men were watching me. "Did Ryan ever talk about his new girlfriend?" I asked.

"Ryan had a girlfriend?" Carl asked. "He never mentioned one to me, but I'm not surprised. He's good-looking boy."

Bobby added, "Ryan kept his work and social life separate."

"Well, thanks again." I pushed the door open and stepped outside. The grey November clouds had darkened. Cold drops of rain struck my face by the time I'd crossed the parking lot to my car. I decided to head home to type up what I'd observed and to read through the file again. I'd plan my next steps and get a fresh start in the morning. Hopefully, by then, I'd be able to think of some angle that the police hadn't already crossed off the list.

The question was . . . *what*?

CHAPTER SIX

I smelled duck cooking and heard voices when I stepped inside the front door. I padded down the hallway in my stocking feet and stopped in the doorway to the kitchen. Dad and Evan were bent over a bowl with their backs to me.

"Now add the nutmeg and we'll give it one more stir. Then, you can lick the spoon."

"Is this really Aunt Anna's favourite dessert?" Evan asked.

"Well, she has lots of favourites. But this is definitely one of them."

They both turned when I cleared my throat. "Sounds like a spice cake in the works," I said. "You're never going to get me to move out at this rate, Dad."

Dad smiled but didn't say anything. Evan jumped off the chair he'd been standing on and ran over to throw his arms around my waist. I hugged him tightly before letting him go.

"My dad's coming for supper," Evan said as he hopped back onto the chair.

I met Dad's eyes. They were signalling me not to say anything about Jimmy or what was going on with Cheri. "I'm going to type up some notes on the case before supper."

"I'll call when we're ready," Dad said.

I could hear Dad telling Evan to keep stirring until he told him to stop as I walked down the hall to the back den. Dad had set up a desk for me under a window looking into the backyard. The scattered drops of rain had turned into a downpour. Rain streaked the glass and the afternoon sky was dark and heavy.

I sat staring outside for a few minutes. The day's interviews played across my mind and I tried to pin down what was making me uneasy. The feeling had been growing all day and I knew I was missing something important.

My laptop was open to a new page and I began typing notes into the Ryan Green file. With any luck, reliving the day's conversations would make the thing I'd missed pop out. Before that could happen, I heard voices in the kitchen and a minute later Jimmy appeared in the doorway with two bottles of beer.

"Thought you could use a sounding board," he said, dropping into the easy chair next to my desk. I could smell his musky aftershave when I reached over to accept the beer. He was wearing a short-sleeved t-shirt and his arm muscles bulged when he leaned forward.

"Tell me something," I said. "How can a kid from a good family with lots of friends disappear one day without anybody knowing anything?"

"It happens." He took a drink and lowered the bottle to his lap. "Maybe more than we know. Have you run out of ideas already?"

"No, but I can't say I've made any progress... yet. What does Chuck Green do for a living?"

"Ryan's dad? He works for the government in policy or something equally as exciting."

I smiled. Jimmy hated any job that involved sitting at a desk and thinking. "Is the Greens' marriage in good shape?"

"Who knows? They put up a united front, but I get the feeling Vanda is a nervous and controlling kind of woman. I spent a good part of every meeting we had when Ryan first disappeared keeping her from losing it. She kept saying it was her husband's fault that Ryan ran away. Chuck was patient with her, but he usually smelled of liquor. His way of coping, I guess."

"What a sad mess."

As if in solidarity, we both lifted our beer bottles to our lips. While I swallowed, I tried to think how to raise the subject of Cheri. I was saved when Evan bounced into the room to get us for dinner.

We didn't talk much as we dug into plates of roast duck, wild rice, asparagus, salad and homemade buns. I didn't think I'd have room left for spice cake and ice cream but I managed two helpings before pushing my plate away.

"Can I wash the dishes tonight, Grandpa?" Evan asked. "Can I, please?"

Dad pretended to think it over. "Only if I get to read you two chapters of *Treasure Island* tonight. Deal?"

"Deal."

"Is Evan staying over?" I asked, looking at Jimmy.

"I have an early morning shift and your dad offered." Jimmy's phone began ringing in his pocket. "Work," he said, and his eyes were suddenly alert. "Must be something up."

He pushed back from the table and went into the hallway. We sat still, listening to the rise and fall of his voice but not hearing what he said. When he came back into the kitchen, he looked directly at me. "A body was found in the woods just outside the town of Carp. Been there a while. Looks to be a male."

My heart dropped. "Ryan Green?" I asked.

"Too soon to tell. Do you want to come along?"

"Sure. I'll get my jacket."

"Maybe an umbrella too. It's still raining hard." He crouched down and opened his arms wide. "Come give me a hug, Evan. I'm going to need a great big one to keep me warm."

• • • • • • • • • •

Jimmy drove about half an hour west of Ottawa and found a parking spot behind two police cruisers on the shoulder of the highway. Bright lights had been strung up near the body, and we walked toward them through an opening in the brush. Rain dripped from the trees but their branches protected us from the worst of it. Even wearing my raincoat and a thick sweater, the dampness went right through me.

We reached a small opening where the body had been partially buried. Jimmy spoke to one of the detectives, named Oliver Sparks.

"How did someone find the body? This is the middle of nowhere."

"A guy was walking his dogs and they started digging before he got to the scene. A couple of farm hounds."

"Lucky for us. We've been searching for a missing seventeen-year-old boy. Could it be him?"

"Hard to say. This guy's not weathered well. Forensics is having a look now."

Before long, a woman dressed in a white jumpsuit that protected her clothes walked toward us. Her shoes were covered by plastic booties. "All done, Sparky," she said to the detective standing with us as she removed latex gloves. She looked at Jimmy and me but didn't ask who we were.

"What can you tell us?" Sparks asked.

"He was shot in the head. By the state of the body, I'd say he's been dead several months." Her large brown eyes didn't show any emotion.

"How old was he?" Jimmy asked.

Her gaze zoomed in on him. "Officer Wilson?" she asked. A smile filled her face like a sudden burst of sunshine. "I didn't recognize you with your hood up." A look passed between them that spoke of other times. "I can't tell his age yet. Do you think you know him?"

Jimmy turned on the charm. "Been a long time, Lucy. You're looking good as ever. We've got a missing grade twelve student and hope this isn't him. You never know."

"I'll give you a call when I have more. I'll be doing the autopsy first thing tomorrow." Her smile was honey warm and as inviting as an open door.

"I'll sit in on that," said Jimmy. He pulled his gaze away from her to look at me. "Sweet, I'll call you as soon as I know something."

"Sounds like a plan," I said, keeping my voice as flat as a pancake. I stepped around the two of them to get a closer look at the body. Two men in white jumpsuits had already loaded it onto a stretcher and were pulling a cover up over what was left of the man's face.

"You won't be able to recognize him," Lucy warned from behind me. "Several months in the woods have not been kind. Hungry wild animals and all that."

I changed my mind about asking to have a look and let them take the stretcher past me without comment. I looked over at Jimmy. "I'll see you back in the car. Take your time if you have other...business to wrap up."

Jimmy sounded amused. "I'm right behind you."

We'd almost reached the road when I said over my shoulder, "Old girlfriend, Officer Wilson?"

"I wouldn't call Lucy old, exactly." Jimmy chuckled. "And she was never my girlfriend, Sweet. I'm a true blue kind of guy."

I choked back my first reply and said instead, "Good to know, because for a minute there, I could have sworn the lovely Lucy thought you had a history together."

Jimmy caught up to me and leaned his head close to mine. "When a woman has a history with me, Sweet, neither one of us ever forgets it."

CHAPTER SEVEN

Dad and Evan were both asleep when I got home. I poured myself a Scotch and snuggled under a blanket on the couch to warm up. Dad had tucked a section of the newspaper nearly out of sight under his chair. I reached over and pulled it out. He'd been reading the arts section, which was unusual. It was the section he normally skipped. He'd folded the paper in two so I opened it and spread out the pages.

Nick's frowning face stared back at me, the gorgeous actress Carolina Mambella close beside him. She was smiling, her long black hair loose around her face. Her lips were painted a startling red, making her black eyes appear even blacker. One of her hands rested on Nick's arm. Her nails were as blood red as her lips. The headline read: *Actor Nick Roma Dating Italian Bombshell Carolina Mambella*.

I sat for a while with the paper in my lap. "So that's that, then," I said. I suddenly felt very tired.

Nick had talked about moving in together before he left to make the movie in British Columbia. I hadn't jumped at the idea but said we could talk about it when he got home. The careful part of me had worried about getting in too deep too fast. I guess that wasn't going to be an issue any longer.

I finished my drink in one gulp and walked down the hall toward my bedroom. I stopped when a scream broke the silence.

Evan.

I took the stairs two at a time and reached the landing in time to see Dad's back disappearing into the guest bedroom. The screaming stopped and I could hear Dad telling Evan that everything was going to be okay. It was just a bad dream.

Dad was rocking Evan in his arms when I reached the doorway. I waited for him to tuck Evan back in and join me in the hall. Dad looked tired and I reached out a hand to pat his shoulder.

"You okay, Dad?"

"As okay as a person can be after being woken up like that. How did it go tonight?"

"Not sure. We'll find out tomorrow if the body they found is Ryan Green." I took one last look at my sleeping nephew. "Evan is having a hard time."

"He's worried about his parents. Can't say that I blame him."

"I'll see if I can talk to Cheri tomorrow."

"I think it's time." Dad ran a hand through his white hair so that it stood on end. "Well, I'm heading back to bed."

"I'm on my way, too."

I didn't mention that I knew Nick had betrayed me with the Italian actress. We'd both had enough upset for one night. And I wasn't sure that I could take Dad's pity even if I only saw it in his eyes.

· · · · · · · · · ·

Dad and Evan were still sound asleep when I left the house in the morning. The rain had stopped, but a northern wind had come up. A chill ran through me as I stepped outside into the darkness. The sun wouldn't rise for another hour or so.

I drove downtown and parked outside the yoga studio where Cheri worked out. She said that she needed this exercise to kick start her days. We all thought she worked too much in her lawyer job, but she wouldn't listen to our concerns. It seemed that becoming a partner in the law firm had started to be more important to her than her marriage. I shouldn't have been surprised. Cheri had always needed to prove herself, even as a little kid. None of us could convince her that she was good enough just as she was.

The class was full: thirty women in workout clothes, arms resting on mats and rear ends stretching up to the ceiling. I spotted Cheri in the front row before I walked two blocks for a takeout coffee. I finished drinking it by the time Cheri came out of her class twenty minutes later. She looked surprised to see me standing on the sidewalk.

"Do you have time for breakfast?" I asked. "My treat."

"No," she tilted her head and smiled, "but I can make time."

We fought the wind down the street to John's Diner and found a booth near the front window. Cheri ordered poached eggs and toast with a glass of water on the side. I went for the full meal deal—scrambled eggs, bacon, potatoes, toast, jam and coffee. I had the feeling it was going to be a long day and that I was going to need the energy.

We both looked out the window for a while, not talking. A plastic bag blew past, followed by a newspaper.

Finally, Cheri turned her head to look at me. "I've asked Jimmy for a divorce. We're too far apart now to make our marriage work."

"But Jimmy loves you."

"I'm not so sure." Her smile came and went. "He loves the girl I was when we got married. But I've changed. I want more than Saturday nights in front of the television eating pizza. I don't want any more kids..." Her voice trailed off.

That was the moment I knew Cheri and Jimmy weren't going to patch things up. They would not have their happily ever after. I wasn't sure how it made me feel. Sad, depressed...*hopeful*? Was this what I'd wanted all along? For Jimmy to come back to me after he realized I was the sister he should have married?

"What about Evan?" I asked.

"We'll be sharing him fifty-fifty for now, although Jimmy has agreed to be flexible if we need to adjust schedules because of work. And there's always Dad."

Always Dad. She didn't seem to realize the strain she was putting on him. But I knew my sister was hurting, too. I reached over and took her hand from where it rested on the table. "I want to make sure you're okay," I said.

"I'll be okay." Her eyes didn't waver when she looked into mine. They were clear blue and determined. Her voice dropped almost to a whisper. "He never loved me like he loved you, Anna," she said. She gave me one more half-smile before gently pulling her hand free from mine.

CHAPTER EIGHT

"It's not Ryan." Jimmy spoke to somebody else and then back into his phone. "Whoever it is was in his forties and was killed by a gunshot wound to the head."

I'd pulled my car over to the side of the road to answer my cellphone. In a strange twist of late fall weather, today was sunny and unusually warm. I leaned my head back against the seat and looked at the blue sky as I asked, "Do you have any idea who he could be?"

"We're going through the missing persons files now and checking his prints with the database."

"You were able to get prints?"

"Only from one hand. The other hand wasn't in good shape...Do you really want to know the details?"

"No, that's okay. I'm going to head over to the Greens to talk with Chuck and Vanda. I was waiting to know if we'd found Ryan."

"Let's stay in touch."

I eased my car back into traffic and continued north on Bank Street. The Greens lived west of Bank on a street filled with large houses on narrow lots. Their house was a three-storey red brick home set back from the road and surrounded by an iron fence. I got the feeling that this was a quiet street with wealthy owners who liked their privacy.

I parked and opened the gate, which creaked loudly. By the time I reached the front door, Vanda Green was holding it open, inviting me in. She brought me into the kitchen at the back of the house. It was completely modern with granite countertops and stainless steel appliances. Green-shaded lamps hung over a large central island. I sat on a stool next to the island while she poured coffee.

"You just missed Chuck and Travis," she said, sitting down across from me. Her hair was threaded with grey and her perm was growing out, curly at the ends and straight in other places. "They've gone to the mall." Her hands moved constantly, pouring cream, adding sugar, tapping her fingers on the counter. "I won't let Travis go alone anymore."

"I know this is a difficult time for your family," I said. "Before you hear on the news, a body was found yesterday evening. But it's not Ryan."

One hand found the buttons on her shirt. "Thank the Lord. Who was it?"

"The police are trying to find out now. It's a man, but he's older than Ryan."

"His poor family."

"Can you tell me about the week Ryan went missing? Did anything unusual happen, no matter how small it seemed at the time? A change in Ryan's behaviour, perhaps?"

Vanda's eyes searched the room as if the answer could be found in one of its corners or behind a piece of furniture. "He was mad at me," she said at last. "We had a fight that morning. Ryan said that he was tired of my constant worrying and I had to give him some room." Her eyes filled with tears. "Did I push him away? I haven't been able to sleep, thinking that I'm the reason he's gone." Her voice dropped. "He yelled awful things. I...I was shocked. I never told anybody, not even Chuck. I was scared the police would stop looking for him. My son would never run away."

"Do you know who his new girlfriend was?"

"Ryan always had new girlfriends. I think he kept this one a secret so I wouldn't check up on her. I did that sometimes."

No wonder he'd told her to back off. I tried a new line of questioning. "You moved around a lot, before settling in Ottawa a few years ago. What does your husband do, exactly?"

"Chuck works for National Defence in the office. He orders equipment. It's boring work, from what he tells me." She laughed and wiped her eyes with the back of her hand. The laugh seemed out of place.

"Where did you live before you moved to Ottawa?"

"Oh, different places. The last posting was in Paris." She waved a hand in the air. "I became ill and we decided to come back to Canada. I wish now that we hadn't."

"Could Ryan have gone back to Paris or one of the other places you lived?"

"Not without his passport. It's in our safe." She stood up and glanced toward the hallway. "Would you like to see his room?"

"Yes, thank you."

She led me upstairs to a bedroom at the end of the hall. It was a large, square-shaped room with a queen-size bed and a desk under the window. Posters of soccer players filled one wall and a collection of model airplanes sat on top of a dresser next to the closet. I carefully searched through Ryan's clothes and books, but I didn't find anything helpful. I hadn't thought that I would. Jimmy and his team would have already been through the room with a fine-toothed comb.

Vanda had left me alone in the bedroom and gone back down to the kitchen. She met me at the bottom of the stairs, wiping her hands on a dish towel. "Did you find anything?" she asked.

"No, but don't give up hope. I won't stop until we find Ryan."

"That's the same thing the police said." She opened the front door and waited for me to step past her. "I'm beginning to wonder if my son even wants to be found. Because the idea that someone is keeping him from coming home is more than I can bear. You will let me know if you find anything new?"

"You can count on it," I said.

I was more determined than ever to find out what happened to her son. Because nobody deserved to live with the pain that I saw in her eyes.

....

I called Dad as soon as I got inside my car. He answered on the third ring with a gruff hello. "Do you have time to do some research for me, Dad?"

His voice lightened. "Of course. What have you got?"

"Chuck Green, Ryan's dad, is in the Department of National Defence, where I know you still have contacts. I need to know more about what he does for a living. He lived overseas for a number of years and moved around a lot. I'm wondering if something in his past could be a factor. I'll send you a text with their address details so you have something to start with."

"Mission accepted. I'm on it. Dinner might be a little late."

"Me too, so that works."

I hung up and checked my watch. I wasn't that far from the Bella Vista Restaurant. I had time to find out why the waitress, Jeannie, had acted strangely and disappeared after I asked her about Ryan. I didn't like loose ends and she felt like a long, dangly one.

CHAPTER NINE

As it turned out, I didn't need to speak with Jeannie after all. She wasn't working the lunch shift but the girl who served my table was happy to talk. As she set a cup of coffee in front of me, I asked, "How long have you worked here?"

She paused and appeared to be counting in her head. "I had my son three years ago and started here the year after that. So two years. Wow, time flies."

"Good place to work?"

She shrugged. "It's okay. I'm starting to get better shifts."

I read her name tag. "Tara, did you know that high school kid, Ryan Green, who went missing six months ago?"

I could tell that I'd caught her by surprise. She looked toward the kitchen and back at me. "Yeah, he used to come in for a burger before his shift." She started to turn.

"Did he always come in alone?" I picked up my coffee cup and took a sip while I watched her.

She turned back. "Why are you asking?"

"I know his family. They're devastated, not knowing what happened to him."

"Yeah, I get it. If something happened to my kid…" She took a step closer. "The last two times I saw him, he met a girl. They took the booth over there in the corner."

"What did she look like?"

"Pretty. Long, dark hair and green eyes, but I can go one better. I know her name." Someone came out of the kitchen and she stopped talking.

"Is there a problem?" I asked.

Tara shook her head, but said, "Jeannie told me to mind my own business if I want to keep my job. So maybe I should listen to her. Forget I said anything."

I had my cellphone out before she made it over to the next table. I looked out the window and said, "Dad, I need you to track down one more person."

· · · · · · · · · ·

Carleton University was on the opposite side of the canal to the Green home and west of Bronson

Avenue. I took the long curving road into the campus and found a parking spot in the first big lot.

With the change in the weather, I didn't mind the walk across campus. A path led me past student dorms and buildings where classes were held. I entered a central bricked courtyard with the library directly ahead. Students criss-crossed my path but nobody was in a hurry. It was as if we all wanted to stay in the sunshine as long as possible.

When I reached the main entrance to the library, I sent a text message. A few minutes later, Maggie Montana joined me on the steps. She was wearing a red leather jacket and carried a binder and a text book. She'd dyed her long hair white and added a purple streak down one side. But her eyes, the same unusual colour as her dad Bobby's, were still green.

"Thanks for meeting me on short notice," I said. "Has anybody told you that you look a lot like your dad?"

"All the time, although his hair is still black." She smiled and I could see why Ryan would have fallen for her. "We can get a coffee if you like."

"Perfect."

We found seats in the cafeteria that were away from the other students. "What are you studying?" I asked to put her at ease.

"History and English. I'm thinking about taking a law degree." Her eyes were puzzled. "Why did you want to see me? The man who called told me this was about my program."

Dad. "I'm sorry if the message got mixed up. I'm actually trying to track down Ryan Green and somebody told me that you were dating him." I didn't expect the flash of anger that crossed her face. "Does his name upset you?" I added.

"You might say. I thought we had something good going on. Then he quit working for my dad and never called me again." She snapped her fingers. "Dropped me like that."

I tried to see if she believed what she'd just said. "You do know he's missing?"

She stared at me and blinked. "What do you mean, missing?"

"Gone. As in nobody knows where he is."

"Since when?" Her voice was less certain.

"He was last seen leaving school on Wednesday, May 30, and hasn't been seen since."

She covered her mouth with her hands and closed her eyes. After several seconds she dropped her hands and looked at me. "I had no idea. My father...nobody knew we were seeing each other. I guess...Dad." She stopped and started again. "My father was mad that Ryan quit work without giving any notice. He wouldn't have known it mattered to me if he found out that Ryan had disappeared.

"It was in the news toward the end of June. Everyone at Brookfield High School was talking about it."

"I didn't go to Brookfield, and I went to stay with my mother in Boston for the summer. I left right after exams because it was the only time Dad had to drive me. He took me out of school a week early."

"Why did you keep your relationship with Ryan a secret?"

"Ryan worked for my dad. It was...awkward."

"Did you see Ryan after school that day?"

"I don't remember."

"His soccer practice was cancelled and he had a few free hours. Are you sure he didn't go see you?"

She shook her head. "I need time to think. Maybe. I could call you later." She stood and picked up her books. "I'm sorry, but I have to go."

I watched her nearly run from the room as I tried to fit this latest piece into the puzzle.

CHAPTER TEN

"Chuck Green is one mysterious dude," Dad said into my ear. "Took some digging but I got some information from an old army buddy. But we have to keep it to ourselves."

"Of course." I shifted the phone to my other ear and put my feet up on my desk. I'd opened a beer when I entered the office and took a sip while I listened.

"Chuck Green was undercover on some mighty dangerous assignments overseas. Last stint, he was spying on a terrorist cell in France."

"He was a government spy?"

"Yes, and a good one, according to my friend. Does this information help you out?"

"It might. Thanks, Dad."

"One more thing. Chuck's wife had a nervous breakdown and that's why they came back to Canada. She knew about the danger Chuck was in and the stress finally got to her. He gave up the spy business and took a desk job. I hear he misses the field work, though."

"Thanks again, Dad. You've helped answer some questions I've had about the Greens."

After Dad hung up, I sat for a few minutes and tried to work out how these latest details might be connected to Ryan's disappearance. I picked up my phone again and called Jimmy.

He sounded out of breath. "I was about to call you. Chuck Green was shot in a parking garage about twenty minutes ago. He's being taken to the Civic Hospital in an ambulance as we speak. I'm on my way there now."

"I'm in my office so I'm not far from the hospital. I'll meet you." *Could things get any worse?*

Ten minutes later, I was circling the hospital trying to find a parking spot. I was lucky to find one on the second go around. I met Jimmy inside the emergency waiting room. He was talking to a nurse but met my eyes as soon as I stepped through the door.

"This shooting puts a new spin on things," he said when he finally came over. "I don't suppose you've found out anything helpful yet, PI Sweet?" The teasing in his voice made me angry. Jimmy had spent six months on the case, and clearly thought that I wasn't going to find anything he hadn't. If I'd been willing to share, he'd killed the mood.

"How bad is Chuck Green?" I asked.

"He's unconscious. A bullet hit him in the back."

"Does his family know?"

"We're having trouble reaching his wife. His son Travis is being picked up at school by one of our officers."

"I'm guessing you don't know who shot him."

Jimmy tilted his head toward me. "You've guessed right. Whoever got to him knew what they were doing. Isolated location and no witnesses. Not even a security camera. If a truck hadn't driven into the garage when it did, the shooter might have finished Green off."

"This was his lucky day then... sort of."

"We did find out a bit about the body found in the bush near Carp, though."

"Who was he?"

"Name was Gord Walters. He was a small-time car thief who disappeared six months ago. His roommate reported him missing. The conclusion back then was that he skipped town."

"So I wonder what happened to make him turn up dead."

"Probably owed somebody money."

I needed to forget Gord Walters for the moment and focus on Chuck Green. I sighed. Whatever was going on with the Green family might have to do with Chuck's past life in the spy business. I had to put my feelings aside and share what I knew with Jimmy. I opened my mouth to tell him at the same moment that an officer arrived and dragged him away. I waited half an hour for Jimmy to return before I gave up and headed out to find my car in the parking lot.

· · · · · · · · · ·

"Nobody joining us?" I asked Dad as he set a plate of chicken and potatoes in front of me.

"Cheri took Evan for pizza. I don't know if Jimmy planned to come over."

"He's not answering my texts or voice mail," I said. I took a mouthful of chicken. "This is so good, Dad."

He sat down across from me and took a bite. His nose scrunched up. "Not bad, I suppose." He reached for the pepper. "I forgot to tell you. Nick Roma called and left a message for you yesterday."

"Oh yeah?"

"He's back in Vancouver after nearly a month in the mountains. He said there was no internet connection where they were filming." Dad looked at me with a steady gaze. "He also lost his cellphone with your number saved in it, so he tried the house. He wants you to call him back at his hotel."

"Great. I'll do that." *Just as soon as the moon turns blue.* I lowered my head and kept eating.

"I wondered if you read that gossip piece in the newspaper. You need to speak with Nick before you make up your mind about him."

"I don't want to talk about it, Dad."

Dad grunted but didn't say anything more about Nick for the rest of our meal.

After I helped clean up the dishes, I sat down at my desk and typed notes into my Ryan Green file. I re-read the file from the beginning and thought about the timeline. Ryan went missing after school six months ago. I thought back to my conversation with Jimmy in the hospital waiting room. The small-time car thief, Gord Walters, had been shot and left in the woods outside the town of Carp about the same time. Were the two events related, or not? Had Ryan somehow gotten himself mixed up in a murder?

I sat thinking over different possibilities while staring out the window into the darkness. That's when my cellphone rang.

CHAPTER ELEVEN

I finished the call and went in search of my handgun, which I kept in a safe in my bedroom. On the way to my car, I called Jimmy again and left a message. I didn't have enough information to raise the alarm at police headquarters, but I'd feel better with Jimmy at my side. I would have liked it even better if Jada was in town for back up.

A cold, gusty wind made the trees sway and leaves swirl across the road. Traffic was light, as if people were snuggled inside their houses, avoiding the grim November night. Stopped at Bank Street and Hunt Club Road, I checked the directions again on my phone. I needed to cross to the other side of the Rideau River and drive quite a ways south. I turned right. Once I was over the river, I took Highway 13, which ran parallel to the Rideau. Twenty minutes later, I turned into Winding Way, a road of multi-million-dollar houses that backed onto the water.

I drove slowly up the street, scanning the house numbers until I reached ninety-two. The Montanas owned one of the larger estates at the end of the block—they had a two-storey yellow brick house with turrets at either end, and a three-car garage. There was big money in selling cars, apparently. The house was set back from the road and a long driveway made an opening through trees and well-tended bushes. The property was nestled next to a stretch of thick woods, yet to be developed.

The gate was open, but I parked on the street a few houses down. Something in Bobby Montana's voice when he called half an hour earlier had sounded forced...as if he wasn't talking of his own free will. The uneasy feeling I had was enough to make me bring my gun and to phone Jimmy. It was making me extra careful now.

The main-floor lights were on. I walked toward them through the darkness, the sound of the wind hiding my approach. The living room window was to the left of the front door. I stepped off the path and dodged branches to look into the room. Carl and Bobby were sitting on the couch with their backs to me. They were looking at somebody on the other side of the room, just out of my sight line.

I moved back from the house and speed-dialled Jimmy again. "It's just past nine o'clock. I'm going into the Montana house. Bobby and his dad, Carl, are inside with somebody else, but I can't see who it is through the window. Come as soon as you get this." I repeated the address and ended the call.

Then I pulled my gun out of its side holster and tucked it into my jacket pocket. I'd be able to draw it quickly if I needed to. I truly hoped I wouldn't need to. My last step was to turn on the tape recorder inside my pocket. The device was strong enough to record a pin drop across the room.

Plants and branches were moving black shapes as I made my way to the front door. Dark shadows played across the glass while I waited for someone to answer the bell. After some noises and thumps inside the house, Bobby pulled the door open. My first thought was that he looked deflated—he was not the cocky man in control that I'd met at the car dealership. His eyes were sunken and he appeared to be in pain. His gelled-back hair showed off a forehead beaded in sweat.

"Come in," he said before turning. That's when I noticed the blood stain spreading down the side of his pant leg, a shocking red against the pale grey fabric. He took a step and his leg buckled. I leapt forward to help him, forgetting for a moment about the danger.

"It's only a flesh wound," said a female voice. "He can handle it."

I looked up, keeping my hold around Bobby's waist. His daughter Maggie stood in the doorway watching us. The gun that she was holding was pointed in our direction.

"Bring him over to the couch," she said. "My dad has something to tell you." Her eyes—the same eyes as Bobby's—had no sympathy in their green depths.

I was as surprised to see her with that gun as I'd been by anything in my life. "Maggie?" I asked. "What's going on?"

"Don't worry, Anna." She stopped talking until I'd eased Bobby onto the couch next to Carl. I stood next to the couch, not sure what she wanted from me.

"I needed a witness." She repeated, "Dad has something to tell you."

The two of them engaged in a staring contest for what felt like hours. Bobby finally broke and looked over at me.

"I might have had something to do with that body you found near Carp." He turned back to his daughter. "You aren't really going to shoot me, Maggie, are you?"

Her eyes were cold and very, very angry. "I will if you don't tell us what you did to Ryan."

"Nothing happened to Ryan."

"I don't believe you." Her voice rose and ended in a sob. "You had him killed!"

"No. No, I didn't. I had no idea he was in the house that night. The two of you were sneaking around behind my back like a couple of..." For a split second, I saw the tough street hood in his eyes. Then he remembered that his daughter was holding the gun. He got control of his anger. "Ryan came out of the house and saw me and another guy teaching someone a lesson."

I looked down at him. "*You* shot Gord Walters?"

"My friend shot him. Not me."

"Why?"

Bobby hesitated before saying, "Walters was stealing from me."

Carl ran a hand through his white hair and looked at him. "I told you that sideline business was going to get us into trouble. But would you listen?"

Bobby's mouth twisted into a snarl. "Shut up, Dad."

Carl's sad brown eyes shifted to me. "My son has a racket going. He takes in stolen cars and strips them for parts. Some he ships overseas. Walters was one of his best thieves."

Bobby raised his arm and made a fist. Before he could jam it into Carl's face, Maggie said, "Don't even think about it, Dad. You've been bullying Grandpa for years, but no more." She levelled the gun at his chest.

"Maggie, no," I said. "This isn't the way to solve anything."

"It's the only way." She kept her arm still, the gun steady. "Dad taught me to shoot. He's always liked guns. What did you do to Ryan, Dad? Where did you put his body?"

"I didn't hurt him."

"Your friend hurting Ryan is the same as you hurting him."

Bobby's face was now creased in pain and his breath was coming in short gasps. "Ryan got away. We couldn't find him. We still can't find him."

"You chased him?" I asked.

"Yeah. Through the woods. But we couldn't catch him."

"You found out Ryan and I were seeing each other when you saw him leave the house that night.

Unless…" Her voice stopped as she appeared to be thinking. "Or did that married waitress you sneak around with tell you she'd seen us together at the Alta Vista? Had you already suspected, Dad?"

"Jeannie told me, but I told her that she was crazy. *My* daughter is a good girl, I said. When I saw him sneaking out of our house that night, I knew she was right."

"And still you let me believe Ryan wanted nothing more to do with me. You told me he quit and wanted me to know he wouldn't be back. How could you, Dad?" Maggie was crying now.

I heard the sound of wind in the hallway. Maggie heard it, too, and our eyes locked.

"It's time to end this before anyone gets really hurt," I said. "And for what it's worth, I think your dad is telling the truth about Ryan this time."

"You don't know what he's like," she cried. Jimmy appeared in the doorway. She turned to look at him then slowly lowered the gun onto the floor. She raised both hands into the air. "I give up," she said. "I couldn't kill him even if I wanted to."

I walked over and picked up the gun while Jimmy handcuffed Maggie. He handed her over to the cop behind him.

"I believe the one who needs to be thrown in the slammer is Bobby Montana," I said, pointing to him on the couch. "But he should go to the hospital first. You also need to arrest a friend of his, who appears to have killed Gord Walters on Bobby's behalf."

"That would be Dougie Rivers," Carl said. He'd pushed himself to his feet and stood next to me. "You can find him at the shop, in the back. I heard Bobby say that a shipment of stolen cars was arriving after supper."

Jimmy looked from me to Carl.

"Carl's okay," I said. "He wasn't part of anything illegal."

Carl smiled at me. "Thanks, young lady. I have to say that Bobby never was much of a son. Now, I know he isn't much of a person, either." He ducked his head away from me, but not before I saw the tears beginning to roll down his cheeks.

I stepped sideways and wrapped my arm around his shaking shoulders. Finding out that you're the father of a killer was a tough truth to accept. Both Carl and Maggie were going to have a long road of healing ahead of them. But at least now, Bobby's strangle hold on the family was broken for good.

CHAPTER TWELVE

Jimmy pulled me aside after the ambulance left with Bobby strapped in the back and a police officer keeping him company. "Just got a call that Chuck Green is awake and wants to talk. Come with me?"

"Of course."

I followed him to the hospital in my car. We rode the elevator in silence and found Chuck's private room at the end of the hallway. A police officer stood guard at his door but let us by after Jimmy showed his ID. The nurse inside the room said not to tire Chuck out, then left us alone with him.

"How are you feeling?" Jimmy asked after moving into Chuck's line of vision.

"Been better, but I'll live." Chuck managed a smile. A thick bandage lay across one side of his bald head, probably cut from his fall in the parking garage.

"Do you know who shot you?"

"No, but I can guess. I have a confession of my own to make. I hope you'll understand why I've done what I did."

I stepped closer to Jimmy. I leaned in close to Chuck's long, droopy face. "You've hidden Ryan away, haven't you?"

His eyes widened before he nodded. "My boy was scared out of his mind. Witnessed his boss and another guy from the garage shoot someone. They saw Ryan before he started running. He hid in the woods before making it to his friend Ben's house. They called me first thing the next morning. I took Ryan to stay with a work friend who lives in the far east end of the city. A friend who knows how to keep a secret."

"You never told your wife?" Jimmy asked.

"No. If Vanda knew, she'd have told somebody. Anxiety makes her talk nonstop. Ryan wanted Bobby to believe he'd run away in order to protect us. Vanda's panic helped with the lie, as you can imagine." He looked regretful. "I hated misleading her, but I had to keep her safe, too, until I figured things out."

"She's not going to be happy with *you*," said Jimmy.

"She might take a while to forgive me." That quick smile again. "I was building up a case against Bobby. Pulled his financial records, started tailing him. He must have found out and tried to shut me up. I'm a little out of practice with the undercover work."

We all turned as we heard voices outside the door. Loud voices. A moment later, the door swung open and Ryan Green burst into the room. Travis and Ben and the police officer were right behind him.

"Dad!" Ryan ran to the bed in a panic. He calmed down when he saw his dad awake and sitting up. "Travis and Ben said you'd been shot and I couldn't stay away. I'm going to testify about what I saw that night, Dad," said Ryan, holding onto his father's hand. "I'm not scared anymore, and it's the only way to keep our family safe."

Jimmy put a reassuring arm across Ryan's shoulder. "We've arrested Bobby Montana and some officers are picking up the other guy now. So your family *is* safe. But you both will be called to testify at their trials."

"Maggie didn't know you were in hiding," I said. "She thought you'd dropped her and only found out yesterday what really happened. She's been very upset."

Ryan turned and looked at me. His black hair was longer and messier than in his photo and his eyes were exhausted. He smiled when he said, "The worst part was thinking she knew what her father had done. I'm glad to hear that she didn't."

"I'm just sorry that you had to go through this."

Jimmy checked his phone. "Good news. Your mom is on her way and will be here any minute."

"I'm not sure I'd call that good news, exactly," said Chuck. "Although maybe seeing Ryan will take her mind off the fact we've been lying to her all this time."

Travis was at the end of the bed. He patted his dad's leg. "This is all on you, Dad. You promised that you'd cover for us, remember?"

Chuck smiled at both of his sons and shook his head. "Seemed like a good plan at the time. Maybe it's for the best that I'm in this hospital bed. Otherwise, I have a feeling I'd be sleeping in the dog house."

· · · · · · · · · ·

"Going to be a long night," Jimmy said as we rode the elevator to the hospital lobby. "I can come by your dad's house to fill you in tomorrow morning."

"A phone call would be enough. You'll be tired."

"I'd like to see you."

"Jimmy..."

He sighed. "It's like this, Anna. Cheri and I are finished. There's no reason you and I can't see each other again."

This was the moment I'd dreaded, and wanted, since I caught the flight home to Ottawa a year before. Our unfinished business had nothing to do with Nick or Cheri. It had always been between Jimmy and me. I took a deep breath. "The reason we can't see each other again, Jimmy, is because I don't want to."

"I don't believe you."

The elevator door opened but we both stood looking at each other, neither of us wanting to back down. Both of us knowing that we were going to have regrets either way.

"I don't want to go back in time, Jimmy. I'm not mad at you anymore and I'll always care for you, but I won't go back." My voice grew stronger and I felt a weight lift from my shoulders. I was going to be okay on my own. I had finally made my decision.

Jimmy stared hard into my eyes a moment longer, then he looked away. He thrust his hands into his pockets and walked ahead of me down the hall. He didn't look back.

"So that's that, then," I said into the empty corridor.

CHAPTER THIRTEEN

Two nights later, I met Nick at Trio, a bar on Richmond Road a bit west of my office in Hintonburg. His plane had landed and Dad gave him my cell number when he called the house. I was downtown at the police station when he reached me and Trio was a familiar meeting place.

Nick was waiting for me at a corner table in the darkened bar, which was lit by flickering candles on high tables. He looked good. Freshly shaved, black hair cut short, the way I liked it. Better than good.

He stood when he saw me and grabbed me in a bear hug. The outdoorsy smell of him made me weak at the knees. I felt his lips on my forehead, my cheek, my mouth. When he let me go, he pulled out a chair for me and took the one beside it. His black eyes never stopped gazing into my face.

"You're looking so good," he said. "I've missed you."

"I've missed you too."

He'd ordered a bottle of red wine before I arrived, and he poured me a glass. We both had a sip and I searched for the words to tell him that he didn't owe me anything. I wouldn't hold him to any promises he'd made before he went away.

"So, I hear you solved a difficult case," he said.

"We did. A man hid his son away after the boy witnessed a murder. He didn't tell anyone why his son was missing. Not even his wife.

"He must have had a good reason."

"He thought he was protecting her."

"You don't appear convinced."

"I would have wanted to know." We locked eyes. "She suffered a nervous breakdown a few years ago, though. Maybe he was taking that into account."

Nick looked to be thinking it over. "People will go to great lengths to protect those they love. Especially if they've done something to hurt them before. Is the son safe now?"

"I believe so. We have enough evidence to put the killers away for life."

After a brief pause, we both started talking at the same time. Nick laughed. "You go first."

I took a drink and set my glass down. "The thing is, I'm beginning to think we've moved into this relationship too fast. Dad still needs me and Cheri is acting crazy. Evan is having trouble in school. You've got an exciting career and I understand if you want to date other women or..."

"Hold up, Anna. What makes you think I want to date other women?"

"I know you've been dating your co-star. I read the papers."

Nick looked puzzled. "Carolina?"

"She's very beautiful."

"Carolina and I are old friends, but that's it. Her boyfriend is a cameraman and was with us on the shoot."

"Oh. But you never called me or even texted."

"We were out of range and I lost my phone with your number in it. I called your house as soon as we got back to Vancouver. I wondered why you didn't return my call. Didn't you get my message?"

"Yes, but I've been busy with the case." *And I've been a fool to believe what I read in the paper.*

He reached across me to his coat on the empty seat. "I wrote you every day but had nowhere to mail the letters. Thought it would be quicker to just hand them over to you."

I took the packet of letters tied with a red ribbon and knew Nick was the real deal. I was out of reasons for keeping him out of my life. I looked back up at his face and into the eyes that saw all of me. All I had to do was take the leap. I set the letters on the table and leaned closer to him.

Nick took my hand in his. "I was thinking of putting an offer in on a house next door to your dad. That is, if you agree. I know you don't want to move out so I thought I could move closer." He smiled. "Share you with your dad, and Cheri and Evan."

I felt a bubble of joy start up from my ribcage and grinned back at him. "If you're buying the Rizzo house," I said, "you've got your work cut out for you. Mr. Rizzo put flowered wallpaper in every room, and that's about all he did to the house after 1960. The Rizzos were especially fond of green and pink."

"I was hoping you could help me out with fixing up the place. That is, when you're not working on a case."

I raised my glass and clinked his. "Seeing as how I plan to spend a lot of my time with its owner, I should be up for trips to the paint store."

"Good." Nick said. "That's good. Because I plan to spend a great deal of time with my new neighbours. I always wanted to be the boy dating the girl next door. Looks like my wish is finally coming true."

ABOUT THE AUTHOR

 Brenda Chapman is a well-known mystery author. The Anna Sweet Mysteries are a popular series in adult literacy and English as a Second Language programs. *My Sister's Keeper*, the first title in the series, was a finalist for the Arthur Ellis Award in 2014. *The Hard Fall* was nominated for the Golden Oak Award in 2014. A former teacher and senior communications advisor, Brenda makes her home in Ottawa.

ALAN DEAN

ALSO BY BRENDA CHAPMAN

In Winter's Grip
The Second Wife
Second Chances
Cold Mourning
Butterfly Kills
Tumbled Graves

Anna Sweet Mysteries

My Sister's Keeper
The Hard Fall
To Keep a Secret
A Model Death

Jennifer Bannon Mystery Series

Running Scared
Hiding in Hawk's Creek
Where Trouble Leads
Trail of Secrets

You can visit Brenda's website at www.brendachapman.ca